Ahwoooooooo!

by YANNICK MURPHY

Illustrated by CLAUDIO MUÑOZ

CLARION BOOKS (New York)

For Hank, Louisa, and Kit
—Y. M.

To Lili, the most hearty, eager, clever cub I know
—C. M.

Clarion Books
a Houghton Mifflin Company imprint
215 Park Avenue South, New York, NY 10003

Text copyright © 2006 by Yannick Murphy
Illustrations copyright © 2006 by Claudio Muñoz

The illustrations were executed in watercolor.
The text was set in 17-point Beo Sans.

www.houghtonmifflinbooks.com

Printed in Malaysia

Library of Congress Cataloging-in-Publication Data
Murphy, Yannick.
Ahwoooooooo! / by Yannick Murphy ; illustrated by Claudio Muñoz.
p. cm.
Summary: After making several unsuccessful attempts to mimic the sounds of other animals,
Little Wolf goes to his grandfather and learns how to howl.
ISBN 0-618-11762-8
[1. Wolves—Fiction. 2. Animal sounds—Fiction. 3. Grandfathers—Fiction.] I. Muñoz, Claudio, ill. II. Title.
PZ7.M9566Ah 2005
[E]—dc22
2004020721

ISBN-13: 978-0-618-11762-8
ISBN-10: 0-618-11762-8

TWP 10 9 8 7 6 5 4 3 2 1

It is night.

Little Wolf sees the moon.

"I want to howl," said Little Wolf. "Teach me how to howl."

"I am sorry, my Little Wolf, I can't right now," said Mother Wolf.

"I have to find leaves to keep us warm in our den."

Little Wolf went to Father Wolf.

"See the moon?" said Little Wolf.

"Yes, I see the moon," said Father Wolf.

"I want to howl," said Little Wolf. "Teach me how to howl."

"I'm sorry, son. I can't. Right now I have to go into the forest and hunt for our food," Father Wolf said. "Why don't you ask Grandfather Wolf for help?"

"I can't. He's still sleeping," said Little Wolf.

"The moon is rising," said Father Wolf. "He will be up soon. Wait until then."

Little Wolf did not want to wait. The moon was so bright. He wanted to learn how to howl right away.

Little Wolf saw Owl swoop down to a branch in the tree.

"See the moon?" said Little Wolf to Owl.

Owl's mouth was full. He was eating his dinner.

"Excuse me," Owl said, swallowing his food. "Yes, I see the moon."

"Teach me how to howl," said Little Wolf.

Owl preened his feathers and said, "I cannot teach you. I am not a wolf. I can teach you how to hoot," said Owl. "*Whooo-who.*"

"*Whooo,*" said Little Wolf.

"*Whooo-who,*" said Owl.

"*Whooo,*" said Little Wolf, but he could not say *Whooo-who.*

"I do not sound like an owl," said Little Wolf. "I do not sound like you. I sound like half an owl."

Little Wolf went to Frog. Frog was in the pond, hopping from lily pad to lily pad.

"See the moon?" said Little Wolf. But Frog did not hear him. He had already jumped to a lily pad on the other side of the pond.

Little Wolf ran around the pond. "Wait," said Little Wolf. "Stop."

Frog hopped and hopped.

Little Wolf finally jumped into the pond. He swam to Frog just as Frog was hopping through the air. Frog landed right on top of Little Wolf.

"This is a strange lily pad," Frog said, sitting on Little Wolf's wet head.

"No, it's me—Little Wolf. Can you teach me how to howl?" said Little Wolf to Frog.

"I cannot teach you how to howl. I am not a wolf. I can teach you how to croak," said Frog. "*Ribbit-ribbit.*"

"*Birrit-birrit,*" said Little Wolf.

"*Ribbit-ribbit,*" said Frog.

"*Birrit-birrit.* I do not sound like a frog," said Little Wolf. "I do not sound like you. Maybe I sound like a frog inside out, but that is all," said Little Wolf.

Little Wolf went to Whippoorwill. She was just waking up.
"See the moon?" said Little Wolf. "Teach me how to howl."
Whippoorwill opened her eyes. She yawned. "Yes, the moon
is very bright tonight," she said. Then she covered her head
with her wing and went back to sleep.

"Wake up! Wake up!" said Little Wolf. "The moon is out. Time to wake up!"

Whippoorwill lifted her head out from under her wing. "I cannot teach you how to howl. I am not a wolf. I can teach you how to sing," said Whippoorwill. "*Whippoor...*"

But she did not finish her song. Instead, she yawned. Then she covered her head with her wing again.

"Wake up! Wake up!" cried Little Wolf. Whippoorwill woke. But she did not lift her head this time. Beneath her wing she finished her song.

"*Will,*" she said softly.

Little Wolf could barely hear her. She had fallen back to sleep.

Little Wolf thought he might never learn how to howl. He kicked at the ground, and a cloud of leaves floated up into the night.

Little Wolf was tired and cold. He went looking for the other wolves. He wanted to lie down with them and keep warm.

Then he saw the large gray back of one wolf curled by a tree. "Grandfather Wolf, is that you?" said Little Wolf.

Grandfather Wolf slowly lifted his head. He turned to Little Wolf and smiled.

"Hello, grandson," said Grandfather Wolf.

"Grandfather Wolf, I am cold. Can I lie down with you?" said Little Wolf. Grandfather Wolf moved over to make room for Little Wolf. He leaned his neck over Little Wolf to keep him warm. He licked Little Wolf's face.

"I taste tears," said Grandfather Wolf. "Were you crying?"

Little Wolf nodded. "I cannot learn how to hoot or croak or sing. I cannot make those sounds," said Little Wolf. "Maybe you could teach me?"

Grandfather Wolf laughed a deep laugh. "I cannot hoot or croak or sing, either," he said. "I cannot teach you."

"You can't?" said Little Wolf.

"No. I am a wolf. Wolves howl. You should howl," said Grandfather Wolf.

"I tried that first. I asked everyone to teach me how to howl, but no one could."

"There is someone who can teach you," said Grandfather Wolf. "He is old and gray. He lives in the woods. He has a grandson who very much wants to learn how to howl. Can you guess who it is?"

"Oh, Grandfather! You are the one? You can teach me how to howl?" said Little Wolf.

"Yes," said Grandfather Wolf. "The moon is full. It is a perfect night to learn how to howl. I will teach you. First you have to sit down and face the moon."

Little Wolf sat down in a clearing and faced the moon.

"Then you have to lift up your head.

"Then you have to stretch your neck.

"Then you have to think of all the things you love,"
said Grandfather Wolf.

Little Wolf thought of all the things he loved.

Playing in the leaves that
Mother Wolf found for their den.

Dinnertime with his
family, sharing the meals
Father Wolf brought home.

Hearing Owl "*Whooo-whoing.*"
Whippoorwill trilling, "*Whippoorwill,
whippoorwill.*" And Frog's croaky
"*Ribbit-ribbit.*"

Feeling the warmth of the other wolves in his pack when he lay curled next to them in sleep.

Seeing the moon. How it made the water in the lake shine. How it made the floor of the forest glow white.

And he loved listening to Grandfather Wolf's deep old voice, teaching him now how to howl.

"These are the things I love," Little Wolf said.

"Now you have to find the howl inside of you," said
Grandfather Wolf.

"Where inside of me?" said Little Wolf.

"There," said Grandfather Wolf, and he nudged Little Wolf's
chest with his nose.

Little Wolf's chest felt warm. It felt as if it was glowing.
It felt as if the moon was shining inside him.
  "Oh, I feel it," said Little Wolf. "I really feel it."
Little Wolf lifted up his head.
Little Wolf stretched his neck.

And then Little Wolf howled.

It was a big howl. It was a huge howl. It was enormous.

"AHHHHHHHHHHHHHHHHHHHHWWWWWOOOOOOOOOO!"

It was a howl that shook the branches in the trees. It was a howl that splashed the water in the lake.

Mother Wolf heard the howl. She stopped looking for leaves and went to see where the howl was coming from.

Father Wolf heard the howl, too. He stopped hunting and went to see where the howl was coming from.

"Is that our Little Wolf howling?" they asked when they saw Grandfather Wolf and Little Wolf together in the clearing.

"Yes. Now he knows how to howl. He is a good little wolf." Grandfather Wolf laughed.

"We're so proud of you," Mother and Father Wolf said as they nuzzled Little Wolf. "Little Wolf has learned how to howl!"

Soon the other wolves came. Shoulder to shoulder, all the wolves sat beside Little Wolf. Then all the wolves lifted their heads to the beautiful moon and howled together.